Damned by Despair

A VERSION BY FRANK McGU

Tirso de Molina (*c.* 1583–1648) was the pen-name oï Gabriel Téllez. Born in Madrid, he studied at Alcalá and became a Mercenarian friar in 1601, rising to important positions in the order. He is thought to have written over three hundred plays, of which eighty have survived, including *El Condenado por Desconfiado, La prudencia en la mujer,* and *Don Gil de las calzas verdes (Don Gil of the Green Trousers).* He also wrote several plays based on the Don Juan legend, including *El Burlador de Sevilla.* Criticised by the Church, he virtually stopped writing for the theatre after 1625.

Frank McGuinness was born in Buncrana, Co. Donegal, and now lives in Dublin and lectures in English at University College Dublin. His plays include *The Factory Girls* (1982), *Baglady* (1985), *Observe the Sons of Ulster Marching Towards the Somme* (1985), *Innocence* (1986), *Carthaginians* (1988), *Mary and Lizzie* (1989), *The Bread Man* (1991), *Someone Who'll Watch Over Me* (1992), *The Bird Sanctuary* (1994), *Mutabilitie* (1997), *Dolly West's Kitchen* (1999), *Gates of Gold* (2002), *Speaking Like Magpies* (2005), *There Came a Gypsy Riding* (2007), *Greta Garbo Came to Donegal* (2010) and *The Match Box* (Liverpool Playhouse, 2012). Among his many widely staged versions are Ibsen's *Rosmersholm* (1987), *Peer Gynt* (1988), *Hedda Gabler* (1994), *A Doll's House* (1997), *The Lady from the Sea* (2008), *Ghosts* (2010) and *John Gabriel Borkman* (2010), Sophocles' *Oedipus* (2008) and Euripides' *Helen* (2009).

also by Frank McGuinness

GATES OF GOLD
DOLLY WEST'S KITCHEN
MARY AND LIZZIE
SOMEONE WHO'LL WATCH OVER ME
MUTABILITIE
OBSERVE THE SONS OF ULSTER MARCHING TOWARDS THE SOMME
SPEAKING LIKE MAGPIES
THERE CAME A GYPSY RIDING
GRETA GARBO CAME TO DONEGAL
THE MATCH BOX

FRANK McGUINNESS PLAYS ONE
(*The Factory Girls,*
Observe the Sons of Ulster Marching Towards the Somme,
Innocence, Carthaginians, Baglady)

FRANK McGUINNESS PLAYS TWO
(*Mary and Lizzie, Someone Who'll Watch Over Me,*
Dolly West's Kitchen, The Bird Sanctuary)

Translations
A DOLL'S HOUSE (Ibsen)
PEER GYNT (Ibsen)
ELECTRA (Sophocles)
OEDIPUS (Sophocles)
THE STORM (Ostrovsky)
HECUBA (Euripides)
MISS JULIE (Strindberg)
PHAEDRA (Racine)
THE LADY FROM THE SEA (Ibsen)
HELEN (Euripides)
GHOSTS (Ibsen)
JOHN GABRIEL BORKMAN (Ibsen)

Screenplays
Brian Friel's DANCING AT LUGHNASA

THE DAZZLING DARK: NEW IRISH PLAYS
(edited by Frank McGuinness)

TIRSO DE MOLINA

Damned by Despair

a version by
Frank McGuinness

from a literal translation by
Simon Bredon

faber and faber

First published in 2012
by Faber and Faber Limited
74–77 Great Russell Street, London WC1B 3DA

Typeset by Country Setting, Kingsdown, Kent CT14 8ES
Printed and bound by CPI Group (UK) Ltd, Croydon, CRO 4YY

A CIP record for this book
is available from the British Library

ISBN 978–0–571–29464–0

2 4 6 8 10 9 7 5 3 1

For Philip Tilling

Damned by Despair in this version was first presented in the Olivier auditorium of the National Theatre, London, on 2 October 2012. The cast, in alphabetical order, was as follows:

Paulo Sebastian Armesto
Celia Leanne Best
Lisandro Jonathan Broadbent
Lidora Lorna Brown
Enrico Bertie Carvel
Escalante Ashley Chin
Albano John Cormack
Anareto Michael Gould
Prison Governor Jonathan Jaynes
Pedrisco Rory Keenan
The Devil Amanda Lawrence
Roldán Tunji Lucas
Roderigo Okezie Morro
Octavio Pierce Reid
Cherinos Dwane Walcott
Galván Alex Warren
Governor of Naples Simon Yadoo
Ensemble Marianne Adams, Anne Bird, Nick Blakeley, Brian Martin

Director Bijan Sheibani
Set Designer Giles Cadle
Costume Designer Moritz Junge
Lighting Designer Jon Clark
Video Designer Finn Ross
Music and Sound Dan Jones
Movement Director Aline David
Fight Director Kate Waters

Characters

Paulo
Pedrisco
The Devil
Octavio
Lisandro
Celia
Lidora
Enrico
Galván
Roldán
Escalante
Cherinos
Anareto
Albano
Roderigo
The Governor of Naples
A Shepherd
A Prison Governor
A Judge
Henchmen
Bandits
Travellers
Wardens
Prisoners
Musicians
Villagers

DAMNED BY DESPAIR

Act One

Two caverns among small crags.
  Paulo, a hermit, enters.

Paulo
  This place of shades – my shelter,
  Saving me, its heat and cold –
  This forest, its loneliness,
  I am blessed and welcome here.
  The green grass and pale shrub.
  The dawn dews the same grass
  Emerald and pure crystal –
  Staining it with mortal beauty,
  The mortal sin of foul beauty.
  I come out from this cave
  That lies in this craggy pyramid
  That nature did create,
  Sister to the shifty clouds,
  Alone keeping me company.
  There is nothing else in the sky.
  The same sky is blue beneath
  The lovely feet of Christ.
  And I know, Lord, you watch over me
  From your luminous throne,
  Served by handsome angels,
  More splendid than the sun.
  How will I, all unworthy,
  Thank you for guiding me so well –
  Grant me grace in this wilderness,
  Give me that glorious victory.
  The rush and the thyme resound

With love of the sweet birds' song.
Their soft airs whisper and caress.
I hear you in their voices –
If such beauty beggars belief on earth,
What wonders are there in Heaven?
The streams are shards of glass
From broken silver mirrors
In which I see my dreams
Lulling me, leading me to sleep,
Suffusing my soul with thoughts of you.
The flowers in the field,
They perfume the passing day.
Their colours play like children
In this fertile meadow,
Astounding, lovely –
More rare than a Moorish carpet.
For this garden of delights,
These joys, these gifts, this goodness,
Bless you a thousand times,
Almighty Lord, Almighty God.
Here will I serve you,
Follow you in word and deed,
For I have left the world behind me.
Madmen hammer at my door,
Distracting me, deceiving me –
Come back to my old ways.
No – divine Lord, I want –
I beg you on my knees
Keep me on this path,
Show me your mercy.
Mankind is made of clay,
Fragile and filthy clay.

He enters a cave.

SCENE TWO

Pedrisco enters with a batch of hay.

Pedrisco
    Look at this boy – a pack horse,
    My cargo green grass
    Hauled from the side of this hill.
    Eat this feed –
    I'll end the sorry man,
    No better than beasts in the field.
    When my ma whelped me into this world,
    These were her words:
    Pedrisco, my pet,
    May I live to see you a saint.
    My granny and aunt agreed.
    Saints, yes – they have the best of luck,
    But a hungry man's hard up.
    Starvation is sinful.
    I'm speaking like a lunatic,
    But then I look like one.
    So, Lord, forgive the lunacy –
    You see the cut of me.
    Don't lose the rag at this request.
    Fill my belly to the brim,
    I'll deafen you with prayers,
    Or I'll pass on being canonised.
    In your infinite wit and wisdom,
    I know, Lord, your love has no limit –
    Let me be a saint that stuffs his face.
    That would be sweet, my Lord.
    Ten years ago Paulo removed me
    From all my kith and kin.
    We moved to this back of beyond,
    He in one cave, me in another.
    It's here we do our penance,

And sometimes they stray into our head –
All the things we left behind us,
And me, I say to the mournful elms
– Why aren't you plates of ham?
Big juicy fistfuls of ham?
Ham was the lad when hunger hit –
Stick your teeth into succulent pig
And grunt all the way to your granny's –
But now my throat's cut with want,
I give birth to the month of May,
My belly one big burst of flowers.
There's Paulo coming from his dark cave.
I want to go into my own pit of darkness
And dine delicately all on my own,
Turning green as this feed of grass.

Pedrisco exits as Paulo enters.

SCENE THREE

Paulo
Sleep is like death, its spitting image,
Cruel, fearful as are my dreams.
A devout man driven to distraction,
I forgot to say my fervent prayers.
Then a strange, similar vision came
Where I enraged eternal God –
Or is it our old enemy, Satan,
Who's making mock with his illusion?
Christ protect me – I've set my eyes on Death,
Terrible, terrible, cursed that I am.
Though I was spared his scythe,
He flattened me with his right fist,
And his bow and arrows aimed at my heart.
I see myself bleeding with his wounds,

Waiting for Mother Earth to devour me.
I gave up the ghost of my own body.
That's when my soul took leave of my senses
And I – I saw – I saw God.
Hide me away from those terrible eyes
That looked on me without pity.
He held a sword righteous, rampaging.
Beside him, the Archangel Michael –
He read out all my misdeeds.
My guardian angel defended me.
And the Great Judge of all the heavens
Who puts the fear of God in Hell,
Our Saviour Jesus weighed me up
And found me sorely lacking.
Christ condemned me to darkness.
I awoke then – trembling with fear – exhausted –
I saw only that I am to blame,
But I do not know where I stand –
Is this some trap the Devil sets?
Does he raise his sword of fire against me?
I do not know why this is happening.
God above, give me a reason.
Will I be condemned, a guilty man,
As this dream decrees I will be?
Will I see you deliver me into
Your most holy, crystal citadel?
You owe me that kindness, my Lord.
I follow the straight and narrow path –
You would not want me led astray, Lord.
What will my end be like?
Will I go to Heaven or Hell?

SCENE FOUR

The Devil enters on the peak of one of the crags.

Devil

    May I be so familiar – to introduce myself –
    I am a man with a mission.
    Ten years I've hounded this holy man
    To pine for what is passing.
    The sweet boy is solid as a rock –
    I cannot make him waver,
    Till today, he starts to doubt,
    And his faith, it's out the window.
    What makes a mighty Christian?
    Serve your God and do good deeds,
    Everything is honky-dory,
    Welcome – welcome to Paradise.
    But this one, this – living – saint,
    He's begun to grow demanding,
    He wants to hear from the boss in person.
    The sin of pride becomes him.
    No better man than me knows that –
    The source of all I suffered once,
    The source of all I suffer now.
    He has no faith in faith,
    And it's all down to a dream.
    Who can doubt that this is sin?
    An open sewer of sin.
    Now this supreme, this honest judge,
    This God, he gives me licence
    To tempt and to seduce him
    With more of my little tricks.
    Will he be a brave little soldier
    And become my flesh and blood?
    He questions God – not good,
    I'd say there might be trouble.
    And it gives me a great idea
    To see if he's mine for the taking.
    Watch me become an absolute angel,
    And give the boy a helping hand,

To dally with me down the primrose path –
To where? – where he may be going.

The Devil becomes an Angel.

Paulo

God of mine, will I be saved?
Almighty God, hasten to my aid.
Incline, Lord, to help me.

Devil

God has heard you, Paulo.
He has seen your tears.
Lose your illusions and dreams –
They are what confuse you.
I am asked to command you –
Go to Naples – at the harbour
You will see a certain man –

Paulo

Your wise words delight me –

Devil

His name is Enrico, son of noble Anareto,
This is how you will know him –
He is tall and elegant, a gentleman.
I can tell you no more –
When you arrive, you'll see him.

Paulo

I would know what to ask him
When I at last set eyes on him.

Devil

You must do only one thing.
See him, and be silent.
Watch what he does, what he says.

Paulo

Is that all I must do?
I don't understand –

9

Devil

    God wants you to observe him.
    Why?
    That man's end will match your own –
    Absolutely your own.

    He disappears.

Paulo

    What mystery is this?
    Who could Enrico be?
    I am dying to see him.
    I am happy and contented.
    He is – he must be –
    A man steeped in scripture.
    Who can doubt that?

SCENE FIVE

Pedrisco enters.

Pedrisco

    A most nutritious dose of grass,
    Quite numbing my hunger.
    Good fortune, God bless you,
    Smiling down on little me.

Paulo

    Pedrisco –

Pedrisco

    My knees fall before you.

Paulo

    You pick your time well.
    We must be off this instant.

Pedrisco

From here? Hold me back.
Where to, Paulo?

Paulo

Naples.

Pedrisco

What? What?
What for, Father? Why –

Paulo

All will be revealed on the road.
Please God, we'll travel safely.

Pedrisco

Will our own there not know who we are?

Paulo

Not one will recognise us.
Who's seen us in this garb?
And we've aged a bit –

Pedrisco

Out of action, indeed, for ten years,
Safe from prying eyes.
People now forgot your face after an hour.

Paulo

My soul is in ecstasy.
I only obey my Lord.
May nothing harm me,
For you send me to find Enrico.
What a blessed creature he must be.
I am happy – blissfully happy.

Pedrisco

With you all the way there, Father.
You go your way, so do I.

Paulo is gone.

But I might chance a quick one
At Horny Juanilla's.
I remember when she lost her eye –
That was some ride.
Come – Roll on, Naples.

SCENE SIX

The Devil stands alone.

Devil
All has started well.
A fool and his soul –
They are soon parted.
May you find what you're looking for.

SCENE SEVEN

The courtyard and open gallery of Celia's house in Naples.
Octavio and Lisandro, two gentlemen, one a dwarf,
are in the atrium.
Lisandro
It's the word about this woman – Celia –
That's what's brought me to her door.

Octavio
What word would that be?

Lisandro
The most discreet whispers suggest –
Well – that Celia is quite the wag,
The wittiest woman Naples has seen,
They say, for the past hundred years.

Octavio

No word of a lie there –
But the same sparkling wit,
It covers a catalogue of crimes.
A way with words – she has that for sure.
Her rhymes rob men of reason.
They kiss goodbye to common sense –
All tongues and tastes are catered for.

Lisandro

Is that true?

Octavio

As true as you are in lust with her.

Lisandro

Well, what I heard – I admit it –
It made me fall a little in love.

Octavio

There's more to her story, Lisandro.

Lisandro

Spit it out, Octavio.

Octavio

A certain young gentleman –
Her latest likely lad –
The nastiest brute in all of Naples –

Lisandro

Enrico – it has to be him –
Son of old Anareto.
Poor crippled fellow –
The past four or five years,
He's been confined to his bed.

Octavio

You have it exactly.

Lisandro

I've heard wind of this bucko –

Octavio

Enrico, the worst ever sprung
From a woman's womb
In the whole history of Naples.
The lady inside these walls,
She bleeds herself dry for him.
When he's bet the shirt from his back,
He's round to her house,
Kicking her into a corner,
Ripping chains and the rings from her fingers.

Lisandro

Poor lass.

Octavio

Same dame can throw a mean dice,
Taking the trousers from her lovers,
Leaving them penniless on the streets,
Soft words their only shelter.

Lisandro

I stand well warned by a good friend –
Better spin some story to get in –

Octavio

Tell her you need a poem –
You'll pay the price of a ring.
A verse to please a lady –
And Celia, she fits the bill.

Lisandro

I think she's in the courtyard.

Octavio

Christ, if Enrico catches us,
We're for the chop, I fear.

SCENE EIGHT

Celia enters, reading a letter, followed by her maid,
Lidora, who notices Lisandro and Octavio.

Lidora
Madam, we are being observed.

Celia
I usually am.

Lidora
What should I do?

Celia
You do as I do – ignore them.
And be fascinated by this –
Isn't it quite a marvel?

She hands Lidora the letter to read.

Lidora
Who is it from?

Celia
This letter – from Severino –
Charming – utterly charming –
What are they doing now?

Lidora
Nothing – why is it charming?

Celia
A lengthy scrawl full of nonsense.
Isn't he a schoolteacher?
Deduct marks for handwriting.

Octavio
Courage, be brave, Lisandro –

Lidora
Why do you encourage him?

Celia
He fancies himself the hero –
He might rescue me
From my fate worse than death.

Lidora
You mean Enrico?

Celia
Enrico will be my death,
If I don't marry –
And marry well.

Lidora
So this Severino –

Celia
Could be my salvation.

Lidora
Do you think so?

Celia
No, but I'm desperate –
A little desperate –
Not that desperate.
Send him something suitable.

Octavio
Up and at her.

Celia
A letter edged with black.

Lidora
Why – who has died?

Celia
I have – from boredom –
Reading this eternal letter.
Do I make a lovely corpse?

Perhaps that's why they've called,
These lads of high renown –
To pay their last respects.

She turns to the men.

Celia
Gentlemen, we spy you.
What can you be looking for?
May I assist your graces?
What do you desire from us?

Lidora
Could it be a plate of pancakes?

Octavio
We dare to venture here
Into the great poet's house,
For like all noble mansions,
There no one is refused entry.

Lidora (*aside*)
Call my lady a poet
And she is anybody's.
He's done his homework.
We're waiting for a reply, ma'am.
But no, not a chirp from her.
Yes, she is intrigued.

Lisandro
Wisest of women, your fame exceeds Homer,
Your wit humbled Ovid.
My friend praises your genius,
He comes with me to plead –
There is a certain lady, married – not happily –
Ignoring my attentions.
Would you write her something?
In return I promise you

A prize for your beauty.
It is my heart.

Celia
Who do you want me to write to?

Lisandro
A lady loved me when I was rich.
Now I have nothing –
She has gotten to a nunnery.

Lidora (*aside*)
A silent order we hope.

Celia
Do you really rate me over Ovid?

Lisandro
A petty rhymester compared to my lady.
She is a poet who wields a true pen –

Celia
And I surpass Homer?

Lisandro
Homer bows the knee, as I do –
He nods, in agreement –

Celia
Then I shall compose my ode.
I call on the gods and all the muses –

Lisandro
Should I write this down?

Octavio
Splendid idea, splendid – pen, paper –

Celia
It is a remarkably insulting idea.
I shall remember all I recite –

I am divinely inspired.
A nunnery, you say?
Let this be her warning.

SCENE NINE

Unnoticed, Enrico and Galván enter.

Celia
In the morning take your book,
The glass wherein yourself must look –
Your young thoughts, so proud and jolly,
Must be turned to motions holy.
Rise at midnight, to your matins,
Read your Psalter, sing your Latins,
And when your blood shall kindle pleasure
Scourge yourself in plenteous measure.
Holy maid, this must be done,
If you mean to live a nun.

Do not turn joy to waste,
Turn instead to bliss,
My sweet kiss
That will forever last.
So sugared, so melting, so soft, so delicious,
The dew that lies on roses,
When the mark itself discloses
Is not so precious.

Enrico has taken Galván in his arms.

Enrico
O rather than I would it smother
Were I to taste such another,
It should be my wishing
That I might die kissing.

Enrico and Galván kiss, then Enrico casts him roughly aside.

After one night
In your loving arms –
I rip you asunder –
Part of my charm.

Enrico turns his sword on Octavio and Lisandro.

Gentlemen, your mission in this house?

Lisandro
The door was open – we walked in –
Looking for nothing –

Enrico
Do you know me?

Lisandro
That's why we're here.

Enrico
Clear out, God damn you.
I swear to Christ, if my temper's roused –
What's with the squint, woman?

Celia
Enrico, to please me, darling –

Enrico
You dare break breath to me?
Vanish – my lady – vanish –
Or you'll get a good hiding.

Octavio
If our being here upsets you,
We'll take our leave –

Lisandro
Are you this lady's brother?
Are you family –

Enrico
Me – I am the Devil.

Galván
And I have my sword in hand.
Flay them.

Octavio
Stop.

Celia
For the love of God, Enrico –

Octavio
We're up to nothing here.
We want the lady to write some letters.

Enrico
You don't know how to write –
Two big shots like yourselves?

Octavio
Contain yourself –

Enrico
I'll contain myself all right –
Where are these scrawls?

He tears Severino's letter.

Call back for them later –
This isn't the proper time.

Celia speaks lowly to Enrico.

Celia
My love –

Enrico
I will rip their eyes out,
When my blood boils –

Lisandro
   No more –

Enrico
   I'm inclined to do as I please –
   If you don't like that, ponce,
   I'll have the legs beneath you –
   Your like never bothered me.

Lisandro
   He threatens us – this tinker –

Octavio
   Hold your tongue –

Enrico
   On the outside you look like men –
   On the inside you are women.
   A hard fist and soft balls –
   Stand up for yourselves.
   Could you better me against this boy?

   He draws his sword.
      Enrico and Galván attack Octavio and Lisandro.

Celia
   Enrico –

Enrico
   Get back –

Celia
   Put a stop to this –

Enrico
   Let no one dare –

Celia
   What are you doing?
   What harm –

Octavio and Lisandro flee.

Lidora

Now that's a lovely sight –
Two fine lads scarpering –

Galván

I gave them one to remember –
Perfect – quite perfect –

Celia

Enrico, what have you done, my love?

Enrico

Nothing much – the tall one is a foot shorter.
That was a good slash.

Lidora

Your guests get a warm welcome.

Galván

I got the small one –
Right in the jerkin.
He's lost a lot of wool.

Enrico

Celia, why the hassle – always the hassle?

Celia

No more hassle –
Calm down, boy.

Enrico

I am blue in the face telling you
I don't like men calling – fancy men –
They do nothing but annoy me.
What do you get from them?
What have they to offer you?
Advice on how to curl your hair?

They're miserable as misers –
They'd take the tights from St Francis.
Why don't you show them the gate?
Why let them into your house?
It's not for want of my warnings.
You have a knack for annoying me.

Celia

You're in top form, aren't you?

Enrico

Clear out of my way.

Celia

Listen, my sweet –
You do know some of these men matter.
Those two gave me this ring and chain.

Enrico

A quick peep, please.
Looks like good stuff –
I'll take this chain.

Celia

The chain?

Enrico

The ring as well.
I'll lay claim to that too.

Lidora

Let the woman keep something.

Enrico

Has she been struck dumb?
Do you have to ask for her?

Galván

This one loves the sound of her own voice.

Lidora (*aside*)
Christ damn us fools –
Fancying such a shower of shits.

Celia
It's all yours for the taking, darling.
And I am as well –
So listen to me.

Enrico
All ears.

Celia
What I want is for you
To take us this afternoon to the harbour.

Enrico
Wear your cloak.

Celia
I'll arrange for food and drink.

Enrico
Hear that command, Galván?
Go and warn the boys –
Today I step out with Celia.

Galván
Will do.

Enrico
Tell them where to meet
Ourselves and the ladies.
Wait for us there.

Lidora
Excellent – three spare men.

Galván
There should be some sport –
Maybe a bit of a barney.

Celia

Should we cover our faces?

Enrico

That's not my intention.
Show your smiles to all and sundry –
Today I want the world and his wife
To know who you belong to.

Celia

Your wish is my command –
We'll go.

Enrico and Galván, about to go, speak quietly to each other.

Lidora

You need your head examined –
Did you hand over all the loot?

Celia

Such a beautiful boy – so brave –
He knows how to use me well.

Celia speaks in a whisper.

So I must let him think –
And don't you forget it.

Lidora

Then there is a method –

Celia

In my madness? Always.
Some fool must pity me someday.
I am ready to be rescued.

The women laugh and exit.

Galván

Have you forgotten something?

Your little promise yesterday?
Aren't you obliged to knife somebody?

Enrico
They gave me good money –
I've spent half already.

Galván
So why are we strolling by the sea?

Enrico
Tell all later – tight-lipped just now.
The lady's bestowed on me a ring and chain.
Aren't we rolling in it?

Galván
I think I'm following you.

Enrico
The poor bastard will see another sunrise,
Happy in his nappy from the cares of the world.
When we've exhausted supplies,
We'll spill the poor babby out of his pram.

SCENE ELEVEN

A view of Naples from the harbour.

Pedrisco
I cannot credit such a story.

Paulo
God's ways are mysterious –

Pedrisco
So, Father, this Enrico and your good self –
You'll come to the exact same end?

Paulo

27

No mistaking the word of God.
His angels told me this.
If Enrico's damned, so am I.
If he's saved, I will be too.

Pedrisco

Well then, this Enrico –
He must be Gospel-greedy.

Paulo

That's what I believe.

Pedrisco

Here we are – the Harbour Gate –

Paulo

Where the Angel told me to wait.

Pedrisco

Here's where there was that drinking den,
Run by your man the size of a mountain.
A bit further on, if I'm remembering right,
Didn't she live there, the big blonde –
The one who looked like a guardsman –
You took quite a shine to that one.

Paulo

Bad thoughts trouble me –
Vile, vile body –
Brother, listen to me –

Pedrisco

I hear –

Paulo

The Devil tempts me with my past sins –

He lies down.

Pedrisco

What are you up to now?

Paulo
I hurl myself on the hard ground –
Now you can tramp all over me.
Spare me nothing, brother –
Stamp me into the earth.

Pedrisco
You're the boss, Father.
I'll do as you desire me.
Am I hammering you hard enough?

Paulo
Harder, brother – harder.

Pedrisco
Does it not hurt?

Paulo
Flatten me – feel no pity.

Pedrisco
What's pity to a man like me?
Why should I feel it?
I'll tramp you from here to Spain.
Just don't bust a gut, Father.

Paulo
Harder – harder.

Roldán (*off*)
Enrico, stop –

Enrico (*off*)
True as Christ, I'll dump him in the water.

Paulo
I heard the name Enrico.

The gang enter, Enrico dragging in a drowned corpse.

29

Enrico
The world is thick with tinkers – why?

Lidora
Stop –

Enrico
Too late – I've drowned him –

Lidora
What are you doing – stop!

Enrico
No cure for it.
Putting you out of your misery –
I'm doing you a great favour, pov boy.

Roldán
What have you done?

He casts the corpse into the harbour.

SCENE TWELVE

Celia organises the business of food and drink.

Lidora
Why did you not put a stop –

Celia
And have him turn on us?
Do you fancy a dip in the harbour?

Paulo and Pedrisco retire to one side.

Enrico
He comes sniffing after charity.
The smell of want sickens me.
I had to stop him shaming himself
In front of me and the whole world.

I held him in my arms, I did,
And landed him in the water.

Paulo
A callous crime.

Enrico
I think that puts an end to his poverty.

Pedrisco
He'd shame the Devil, that boy.

Celia
Is your heart always so hateful?

Enrico
Keep your mouth shut –
Or you will head in the same direction.

Escalante
For the love of God, let this rest.
Enrico, grab a pew, old pal.

Paulo
They called that man Enrico.

Pedrisco
It has to be another.
Would you choose to be that savage?
He has the singed smell of Hell.
Hold your tongue, see what happens.

Enrico
Take the weight off all your feet,
I want conversation.

Escalante
Heed the man.

Enrico
Celia, here – sit.

Celia
I will, yes.

Escalante
Lidora, beside me.

Lidora
That's my plan, Escalante, sir.

Cherinos
Roldán, next to me.

Roldán
All yours – now and for ever, Cherinos.

Pedrisco
Fine specimens of shite-hawks, Father.
Draw near – hear what they're up to.

Paulo
Enrico – my Enrico – will he not come?

Pedrisco
Shhh – watch what you say.
We don't have a bean and he's hard as nails.
Mind he doesn't duck us in the sea.

Enrico
Time for tall tales, gentlemen –
I want to hear of your mighty deeds,
And you know what I'm referring to –
Knifings, thieving, larceny and lynchings –
Perhaps a little strangulation –

Escalante
Spoken like a gentleman, Enrico.

Enrico
Whatever bad-assed bastard
Makes me laugh the loudest –
Hand him over the laurel wreath,
Sing psalms for his salvation.

Escalante
That's my man.

Enrico
Lead off, Escalante, please.

Paulo
Does the Lord allow such things?

Pedrisco
The way the world works – listen and learn.

Escalante
I'll make a start.

Pedrisco
Smarmy, smug git –
If he was sugar, he'd swallow himself.

Escalante
I've helped twenty-five sinners to Heaven,
Nicked from six or seven houses,
And this boy – this dear dancing dagger –
It's done the dirty thirty times.

Pedrisco
I'd leave you dancing at the end of a rope.

Celia
And you, Enrico, what have you done?

Enrico
Listen, one and all –

Escalante
And not a word of a lie –

Enrico
I am a man who has never told a lie.

Galván
We know – we know –

Pedrisco

Are you hearing all this, Father?

Paulo

I'll just check if my Enrico is coming –

Enrico

I command your complete attention –

Celia

The floor is all yours.

Pedrisco

Listen to the blessings he'll bestow on us.

Enrico

I was born a bad boy – the world's worst –
The proof of that pudding is in this telling.
My wish was my command in Naples.
He was not a knight nor of noble blood,
But my father was rotten with money.
And that's what matters – money – in this world.
As a toddler, I was the right tearaway –
That's how he reared me, quite the wild child,
Loaded and laden and spoilt to distraction.
Oh my papa, to me you were so generous.
I left your chests empty as coffins,
Stripping you bare of hard cash and bling.
You could say I gambled – I would go further –
I took to the dice like a duck to water.
It was my father and mother and family,
The flesh and blood of all my evil,
Leaving me starving, broke and homeless.
Breaking and entry – that beckoned next.
Cheap keepsakes I nicked went on the cards.
I found my honour again among thieves.
We were all adept at the same art.
Seven houses we cleared of their contents,

Sending their owners to kingdom come.
What we stole fed our strange habits,
Five of a kind, until four were nabbed.
No one pinned me down as a culprit,
Though they were put to the rack and screw.
Not a single man ever squealed.
I see the square where they hanged like dogs
And learned my lesson. Work all alone.
Each night I'd trot to the gambling house,
Wait at the door, polite as you please,
Asking for a little protection – know what I mean –
From the jammy buggers who had the luck.
They'd dip their paws into the purses,
Looking for pennies to palm me off.
There was the innocent knife in my hand,
All of a sudden it shone in their belly.
I did not spare the lovely ladies –
Hand over whatever you're hiding,
Or I'd carve my name on their faces –
A portrait of the artist as an animal.
Whose blood stained this steel? Thirty men – more –
I have removed them all from this world.
I turned ten to dust to pass the time,
And as for the other twenty or so,
I must have earned a tidy sum –
Measure it out in dainty doubloons.
You claim this is the clippings of tin –
That's true, but I swear to God,
When I had not the nails to scratch myself,
I'd kill for nothing those nearest to me.
I did the dirty with six foolish virgins –
How did I find six in this filthy world?
Luck must be smiling on little me always.
I did get a stiffy for a married lassie
And entered her house to relieve myself.
She saw, she squealed, she roared for her old man –

35

Incensed, we indulged in fisticuffs.
Seeing him helpless, I gave him my hand,
Hurling him from the high balcony,
And he fell to the floor, dead as a doornail.
The witch, she was screeching – the wronged wife.
I took my knife – stabbed her five – six – times.
That pale breast was now red as ruby –
Her blood in a beautiful scarlet stream,
Freeing her soul, breathing her last.
I've sworn lies to the highest heavens,
Perjured myself for the pure pleasure.
One priest wanted me to amend my ways –
I gave him such a clout in the snout
He dropped half dead before my two feet.
I came across one poor old codger –
He'd sheltered a man he should not have –
I put a match to his humble abode.
All hands inside were burned to a cinder,
Including two kids – brothers, I was told.
I'm a firm believer in effing and blinding –
That's how to make Baby Jesus bawl.
When it comes to Mass, am I regular?
In deepest danger, do I fall to my knees,
Roaring for a priest and the help of God,
Confessing my crimes for the world to hear?
Never, never, never, never, never.
I would not piss on beggars were they on fire –
You saw earlier how I pity the poor.
I avoid like plague priests and pastors.
I've ripped asunder the veil of their temples,
Stolen six chalices, stripped their altars.
The rule of law is a large joke.
A thousand times it's tried to tame me.
I shot the sheriff and the deputy.
They do not dare try to arrest me.
Last, but not least, I am held captive,

Captive to Celia, her beautiful eyes.
She is here, and all respect her,
Because of me, for I adore her.
Whenever she has a stash of money,
She hands it over, though it's not much –
I trouser it for my old father,
You already know him – name of Anareto.
He's nailed to his bed – crippled five years –
And my heart, it breaks for him,
Because he has nothing, that good old man.
I am the sole cause of his present state –
As a youngster I gambled his goods and chattels.
Every word of this is true as a Gospel.
I swear to God – and I do not lie.
Judge among yourself who should get the prize.

Pedrisco
That man should go into politics.

Escalante
No contest, you win the prize –

Roldán
Hands down –

Cherinos
All agreed.

Celia
I crown you with the laurel wreath.

Enrico
Celia, may you thrive a thousand years.

She puts a laurel wreath on Enrico's head.

Celia
Here you go, my darling –
And now, we must dine.

Galván

Best suggestion yet.

Celia

Bravo, Enrico –
Do we agree?

Company

Bravo, Enrico, bravo, bravo,
Long live the son of Anareto.

Enrico

Calm, calm – my party animals,
Now, I let you off the leash.

The gang exit, howling.

SCENE THIRTEEN

Paulo

This evil man, Enrico –
I've just seen him.

Pedrisco

Can this have happened?

Paulo

That is the man the Angel described.

Pedrisco

Is that true?

Paulo

The son of Anareto –
That's the man you seek –
That's what he told me –
That's who this is.

Pedrisco

Alive, he's burning in Hell already.

Paulo

Almighty Lord – Eternal Lord –
I lived in the desert for ten years –
I drank dirty water and fasted on grass,
So that you, most merciful, righteous, wise,
That you would forgive my sins, Lord.
That has changed, changed utterly.
I must go to Hell.
Its greedy flames graze on my body.
I am already in torment.

Pedrisco

Have patience –

Paulo

Damn patience!
I know I must go to Hell,
Into the heart of eternal darkness
That will last as long as God lasts –
Pain without end, souls always burning,
Tortured and tossed in pitch blackness.

Pedrisco (*aside*)

The sound of him scares me.

He turns to Paulo.

Pedrisco

Father, we'll head back to our hillside.

Paulo

I intend to head back there –
But not to do penance.
What would be the point?
If this man's saved, I am saved –
If he's damned, I am too.
We are brothers under the soul –
So fair exchange is no robbery.

Pedrisco

Well spoken, Father –
A smart conclusion.

Paulo

There are bandits hidden in the hills.
I'll enlist in their evil number.
I'll match Enrico in mad badness.
So we're damned, both of us, are we?
Then I'll be revenged on the whole world.
Lord Christ, who'd believe it comes to this?

Pedrisco

We'll hang our habits from the tall trees.
Swank ourselves up a bit –

Paulo

Look on me and fear what's coming –
I curse the world and all its works.

Pedrisco

How will we manage with no money?

Paulo

The Devil himself will provide –
And I'll grab it.

Pedrisco

We'll go then.

Paulo

Forgive me, Lord, for lashing out,
But you've already condemned me.
Once you've given your word,
There's no going back on it.
Since that's so, I want to enjoy this earth
Now such a sad end's in store.
I'll follow, Enrico, where your feet lead me –

He exits.

Pedrisco

> Up to your armpits in the holes of Hell,
> And me planted firmly beside you.

The Devil appears.

Devil

> The source of all I suffered once,
> The source of all I suffer now –
> Yes, the sin of pride becomes him.
> God has heard you, Paulo –
> He has heard you clearly.

SCENE FOURTEEN

The street.

Enrico

> Christ damn this gambling lark –
> It's cleaned me out.

Galván

> You're not the luckiest of men.

Enrico

> I can't clean up playing straight.
> If I cheat, I'm still shot down.

Galván

> You got that money for nothing –
> Why the whine in your voice?

Enrico

> It lasted so little time –
> Have you ever seen the like?
> Luck's like a whore's kecks – never changes.

Galván

> You're enjoying this escapade –

Takes your mind off the main business.
Albano – you have to kill him.
That's the deal with Laura's brother.
Roderigo's paid you up front half of what's owed.

Enrico

I'm skint as a skunk –
I will kill Albano.

Galván

What about other matters tonight?
The boys needs a helping hand, Enrico –

Enrico

I've not forgotten – I'm in with them.
All for one, one for all.
They plan to help themselves, don't they?
At his house, Octavio, the Genoese git?

Galván

Right – in all respects.

Enrico

I'll be first man over the top –
I like to lead from the front.
Tell them I'll wait for them here.
Go.

Galván

There before you know it – I'll tell the lads.
You are the boss, Enrico – some boy.

He exits, leaving Enrico alone.

SCENE FIFTEEN

Enrico

The boys, the lads, the lords of the night,
Wrapped in its shroud of dark sky,

That's how they will come to me.
Till then I want to see my father,
Confined as he is within these walls.
Five years now he's crippled in bed,
And he means all the world to me.
This lost lamb may be a roaring lion,
But I fork out for all his necessities.
Whatever Celia can hand me over,
Or what I take from her, like it or not,
I carry it hotfoot to this house
To give his life a bit of light,
Since he is nearing the end of his days.
No matter what risk I set for myself
Or the fear of God I put in me,
The stealing is all for his sustenance –
I will go without myself, sometimes.
In my hideous and hateful life,
I lay claim to that one virtue –
And I'll go down defending this –
A son should be faithful to his father –
Most sincere, most serious debt.
Never once in this life did I cross him.
Honour thy father – my one commandment
From the day and hour I was born.
My antics and my acting up –
Boys will be boys, don't you know? –
He found out nothing, absolutely nothing.
I know if he had, what would I have done?
There's bone in the marrow of my bones,
And my heart is harsh as a mountain,
But I would have broken and roared like a bear –
I am sorry for all I have done.
I've spared him the grief I've caused others –
I've saved him from hearing my sins.

SCENE SIXTEEN

A room in Anareto's house. A door to a bedroom in the rear, with curtains drawn. Enrico opens the curtains to the bedroom. Anareto is asleep in a chair.

Enrico

This is him – I want a good look.
Is he sleeping? Father?

Anareto wakes.

Anareto

Enrico, my dear.

Enrico

I've been absent too long – am I amiss?
Can you forgive me, Father?
I wouldn't want to anger you.

Anareto

I'm the happy man to see you.

Enrico

You're a sight for sore eyes,
Welcome as the sun in the morning
Warming the city of Naples.
Let me kiss your white hair –
It shines bright as the same sun,
And it's worth more to me.

Anareto

Look how you thrive, my big son –
Long may you last, beautiful boy –
Do good and prosper.

Enrico

Have you had a bite to eat?

Anareto

Me? No.

44

Enrico

You're hungry – you must be.

Anareto

I set eyes on you and forget my supper.

Enrico

You can't eat your love for me, Father,
Large and all as that is.

Anareto

You'll wear yourself out worrying about me.

Enrico

Some food for you, Father –
Wrapped up nice and neatly.
See – I do my damnedest for you.

Anareto

Bless you, sweet Lord, for your bounty –
You have given me such a good son.
He is my feet and my hands,
Now I've no power in either of them.
Help me rise.

Enrico

Father, I want to help you.

Anareto

Your arms are strong as mine were.

Enrico

I wish I could kiss them back to life – life –
Father, you are ill – so very ill.
I cannot stop you dying.

Anareto

Down to God's will – accept it.
The cold is very cold.
All of a sudden I feel it.
I need a sleep –

Enrico

Then sleep –
I'll fetch your clothes –

Anareto

Each time I set eyes on you, Enrico,
I always fear it's the last time.
This disease is devouring me.
And I would like – I have to say this –
I would want you to find a wife.
Then I'll die happy.

Enrico

All I do is to please you –

Anareto

Never doubt a woman's love –
If you do, she will prove you right.
Be of one flesh with your bride –
Love her, obey her, be generous.
Don't wear her down with jealousy.
A woman worth her salt needs no scolding –
Hide your heart until the time is ripe.
That's when –

He falls asleep.

Enrico

Sleep has hit him, as it must,
And he stops in mid-sentence,
Just when I might have learned something.
I'll cover him tight and let him rest.

He covers his father well.
Galván enters.

Galván

Everything is shipshape –
Look down the road –
He's coming – Albano.

Enrico
Who?

Galván
Albano – the man you must kill.
Are you bottling out?

Enrico
Galván, do you see these two eyes?
Shut in sleep – were they to open,
They would frighten me to death.
My name goes before me –
I know too well its full renown,
But where this man lies sleeping –
I do not dare commit this crime.

Galván
Who is he?

Enrico
A great man, most eminent,
The one I fear – the only one
I recognise in this life.
A good son respects a strong father.
If he were my shadow, I would cease
From all the crimes that condemn me.
The sight of him would stop me in my tracks.
Draw that curtain –
I see him and I become a man
Too inclined to mercy – my courage wanes –
I need get back my will of iron.

Galván closes the curtain to the bedroom.

Galván
They're drawn.

Enrico
Now he's out of sight, he is out of mind.

Galván, we can knife whoever needs be –
The whole world and all within it.

Galván

Look out – here comes Albano –
The one that best be sent on his merry way.

Enrico

He's coming courting death – he's found him.

Galván

No denying that.

They exit.

SCENE SEVENTEEN

A street.
Albano enters, followed shortly after by Enrico and Galván.
Albano

Look at the sun – as old as myself –
It's setting and day's growing dark –
My wife, she will be worried –

He exits.
Frozen, Enrico watches him.

Enrico

My hand – hold back – back –

Galván

What's keeping you, Enrico?

Enrico

Who am I looking at?
Who does he resemble?
That shadow of a man,
The image of my father.

48

Tell me should I be cruel now,
Add insult to injury
And piss on all I honour –
No, Albano is ancient.
Kill him, I'd kill my father –

Galván
By Christ, you've lost me there.
You're not the man I once knew.

Enrico
I'm not short of guts –

Galván
You could have knifed him –

Enrico
That is not what I want.
I fear neither man nor beast.
If I'd known Albano was so very old,
I'd never have taken on this job.
Laura's brother could have done it himself.
I make the effort to esteem –

Galván
And your esteem will cost you –
Albano is not a dead man.
That money you were given, give it back.

Enrico
Maybe.

Galván
What do you mean, maybe?

Enrico
What I say – maybe –
If it tickles my fancy.

Galván
He's on the warpath – Roderigo.

Roderigo enters.

Roderigo

I've just set eyes on Albano –
He's hale and hearty as I am.

Enrico

True enough.

Roderigo

Did you not promise to remove him?
Quick to take the money – slow to take his life –
Are you a man of your word?

Galván

He's looking to get a knife slapped in his face.

Enrico

I don't kill old men, your honour.
If that offends, feel free to do it yourself.
And thanks very much for the wages paid –
A wonderful deal all told.

Roderigo

You must give me back my money.

Enrico

Go with God, your grace.
You wouldn't want to see me roused,
Because I swear to Christ above –

Roderigo and Enrico fight with their swords.

Galván

Look at them at it – hammer and tongs –
Satan never sleeps.

Roderigo

My money – I must have it –

Enrico
Mine – entirely mine – eternally mine –

Roderigo
Coward – filthy lackey –

Enrico
Liar –

He wounds Roderigo.

Roderigo
He's killed me –

He falls.

Enrico
Now, who's the sorry sausage?

Galván
He should have stayed in his bed.

Enrico
I kill bad brutes like you, not old men.
Their kind words crack the hardest nut.
If you want proof of that, pup,
Ask God to bring you back to life –
And I will kill you time again.

SCENE NINETEEN

The Governor enters with a crowd of Henchmen.

Governor (*offstage*)
Bring him down – arrest him –

Galván
Not good news, pal –
A hundred men on your trail –
And the Governor in person.

Enrico

 Pile it on – six hundred more.
 If he arrests me, I'm a dead man.
 Show my claws, I might save my skin.
 I want to go down fighting.
 Hello, boys, it's Enrico – come close, you pack of
  cowards.

Galván

 They have you circled completely.

Enrico

 Doesn't that make a pretty picture –
 Pity I have to break through them.

Galván

 I'm right behind you.

Enrico

 What did he say, Julius Caesar?
 Romans and countrymen, lend me your earrings –

 Enrico and Galván attack the Governor and his men.

Governor

 Are you a devil?

Enrico

 I'm just not too keen to kick up the daisies.

Governor

 Then give yourself up – I'll see no harm –

Enrico

 That's not my plan – you have to arrest me –

 They fight.

Galván

 You're yellow as shit.

Enrico continues to attack the ministers of justice.
The Governor gets in the way and Enrico strikes him.
The Henchmen let Enrico and Galván escape as the
Governor falls into his men's arms.

Governor
Christ, he's stabbed me –

First Henchman
He's killed the Governor – Jesus –

Second Henchman
His blessed mother protect us all –
Christ, her son, protect us –

The enormity of this killing stills the crowd.

SCENE TWENTY

Enrico and Galván are on the run.

Enrico
Earth, were you to open and swallow me,
I still could not make my escape.
Ocean, you matched me in our swelling pride,
Now let me drown in the deepest sea.
Great God, have mercy on my soul.
Black with sin, I never stopped believing –
My faith in you is all I hold holy.
Listen to me – what am I saying?
Do I afflict a miserable man?
My sad father, I will bring him with me
From burning Troy, another Aeneas –

Galván
What are you ranting? Stop it –

The Devil's voice is heard off.

Devil

This way – follow me –

Galván

Save your bacon.

Enrico

We can't get out of here by foot.

Galván

Then the water is our getaway –
Throw ourselves into it.

Enrico

Father dear, it breaks my heart to leave you –
I cannot carry you in my arms,
But I do so in my heart and soul –
May I be buried beneath the waves.
Follow me, Galván.

Galván

I am following you –
What's keeping you?
Fall with me.

Enrico

Forgive me, Father.

They plunge into the water and fight against the elements to survive.

Interval.

Act Two

SCENE ONE

A forest.
Paulo and Pedrisco enter as bandits.
There are other Bandits, holding three Travellers
captive.

First Bandit
To you, and you alone, mighty Paulo,
Each man here has sworn his allegiance –
We wait now on your verdict.
These three, do they live or die?

Paulo
Their money – did they hand it over?

Pedrisco
We never got a whiff of it.

Paulo
Then what are you waiting for, fool?

Pedrisco
We did extract it eventually –

Paulo
But they didn't give freely?
I'll now pass sentence.

Pedrisco
I'm all agog.

First Traveller
Show us mercy –

Paulo
Hang them from that oak tree –

55

Three Travellers
Sir – Sir – Sir – Master –

Paulo kicks them as they run to him, pleading for mercy.

Paulo
Does it shock you, this cruelty?

Pedrisco
Nothing shocks me any more.
Was it yesterday I saw you, sir,
A hermit in permanent prayer,
Nearly starve to death, crazed with love of Christ,
Assuring him you lead your life
In the greatest penance, hidden in this forest?
And here you are today, a man of violence,
The boss of these brutal outlaws,
Killing those who cross your path,
Stealing all their money.
What do you expect – me to be shocked?
That's dead and buried – in the past now.

Paulo
I will match Enrico in all his mayhem.
I would even like to leave him standing.
Lord, if I offend, forgive me –
But if we share a single fate,
Then that's the way – I know what I'm doing.

Pedrisco
The blind man walking backwards,
I know what I'm doing.
That's what he said when he fell down the stairs.

Paulo
My eyes are breathing fire.
Each man and beast from here to Naples,
Know in my pomp and pride I'd wreck Heaven.

I see you, trees – talons, feathers,
A rare bird am I, living 'neath your branches,
I will do unto you terrible injury.
To make my name, I'll turn nature unnatural.
Each bush that gives us gentle fruit,
I'll grow there a harvest of human heads
That will outlast each summer and winter,
And more – more – I'd do more if I could.

Pedrisco

I hear your sore heart –
The fires of Hell are warming to welcome you.

Paulo

Hang them all – hang them high – this instant.

Pedrisco

Don't hold me back –

First Traveller

Sir – Master –

Paulo

Not one word out of you to me –
Unless you want to suffer worse.

Pedrisco

Come here to me, all three of you.

Second Traveller

Christ, pity us.

Pedrisco

So I'm the man who leaves them dangling –
I suppose you might say that it's good practice.
I'll know all the tricks of their trade,
When they show up to put me down.

Pedrisco leaves with the Travellers and all but two of the Bandits.

57

Paulo

If we're up to our necks together,
And you stand condemned, Enrico,
Then you must take me down with you.
I never intend to leave your side.
The angel decreed we're on the one track.
When God sends us spinning into Hell,
We'll have done plenty to deserve it.

A Voice is heard singing.

Voice

Mercy is the grace of God,
Absolving every sinner.

Paulo

Whose voice is that?

Bandit

The trees are thick here, sir –
They stop us seeing who it is.

Voice

Repent and stand before the Lord –
His love is pure forgiveness.

Paulo

You two, climb the hill and see –
It must be a shepherd singing.

Bandit

We'll do that.

They exit.

Voice

If you but ask Almighty God
For pardon and for pity,

He welcomes you with open arms,
Most sorrowful and sinful.

SCENE THREE

*A young Shepherd appears on the brow of the hill,
making a crown of flowers.*

Paulo
Sweet shepherd, come – come down to me –
God knows your voice is touching,
Although your words confuse me.
Who taught you that strange air?
I hear it, and I do fear it,
For you seem to sing my soul.

The Shepherd sings.

Shepherd
I believe, believe in God –
Believe without question.
He is master of all mercy,
Master of all mercy.

Paulo
If my sins darkened the sky,
Darkened the seven seas –

Shepherd
Master of all mercy,
He is master of all mercy.

Paulo
If my sins drench the moon,
If they devoured the stars –

Shepherd
Master of all mercy,
He is master of all mercy.
God the Father

Breathed us from dust.
Glorify him
For our free will.
Body and soul,
Beg forgiveness.
He shed his blood
We might be saved,
Washing sinners
Clean of all stain.

Paulo joins in the Shepherd's song and they sing in duet.

Duet
Spotless is she
Without blemish,
Virgin Mary,
Mother divine
Who carried him
Nine months in the womb,
Christ our Saviour,
Redeemer King.

The Shepherd sings alone.

Shepherd
A lamb has been lost –
That's who I look for –
This crown I made
For her lovely head.
This he commands,
My master, my Lord –
He longs to see her
Return to his fields.
Beg forgiveness
If you did offend,
Mercy is waiting,
Mercy for the world.

Turn to him for mercy,
He is master of all mercy.

Paulo

Wait, shepherd – don't go, wait.

He escapes through Paulo's hands.

Is he human? No, he is divine,
In his strange way he warns me,
Shepherd, you only distress me more.
God doles out mercy in half-measures.
That's not enough to save my soul.
Both of us are damned in Hell, Enrico.

SCENE FOUR

Pedrisco

I bring news to take your breath away –
You'll think this is a lie – I swear it's not –
But the strangest thing you could imagine.
You know the green banks and the rough rocks
Where the water falls like a battering ram –
Didn't myself and Celio hear a voice
Disturbing the peace, shouting, 'I'm drowned.'
When we look down, we saw two men swimming –
One with his sword clenched in his teeth –
We did the decent thing and went to save them.
The sea, it was raw – ravenous for blood,
Screaming out that it would swallow them.
First it was flinging them high as the stars,
Then it was dragging them ever downwards.
The waves made it look they'd had their heads chopped,
The two lads struggling in the water.
But they were tough men – made it ashore –
To get to the point – one's Enrico.

Paulo
You saw him?

Pedrisco
I saw him.

Paulo
What did he do when he made it?

Pedrisco
Swore himself purple, cursing Christ –
That's how he thanked the God who helped him.

Paulo
And this is the man God will save, shepherd?
I am losing my reason – what little is left.
Now I'll find out what he wants to do –

Pedrisco
Your men are fetching him.

Paulo
Listen to what you have to do.

He draws Pedrisco aside to talk in private with him.

SCENE FIVE

*Looking wet, and with their hands tied, Enrico and
Galván enter, led by Bandits.*

Enrico
Where are you hauling me like this?

First Bandit
Wait for the boss to give you an answer.

Paulo (*to Pedrisco.*)
Do exactly as I say.

Paulo exits.

Pedrisco
Thy will be done.

First Bandit
Is the boss departing?

Pedrisco
He is.
What were you two gentlemen up to?
Kinda dangerous walking on water.
Have you an answer for me?

Enrico
Go to Hell.

Pedrisco
You're run off your feet arriving there –
Hold your horses – the Devil is kind –
He'll give you a hand on your journey –

Enrico
I would not want to be beholden.

Pedrisco
Spoken like a gentleman – very smart.
Why thank the Devil for doing his job?
What name do you go under?

Enrico
I am called Lucifer –

Pedrisco
Lovely.
That's why you're cooling down in the sea –
After sweating too hard in the fire.
Where is it you hail from?

Enrico
If the wind and water hadn't drained me –

If I'd not thrown my sword in the ocean –
The back of my blade would answer you.

Pedrisco
Do you not realise you're in my power?
You're a brave little mite, but I'm braver –
I've murdered a fair few slugs of wine –
See these hands – rough enough to snuff out a candle –
I've trimmed the wings of many wanton flies.
So you're bad, well, I'm much badder –
Nasty old Nick – that's my name –
And I swear to good God –

First Bandit
Give it to him, Pedrisco – go for it –

Enrico
How long do I listen and say nothing?

Pedrisco
As long as you'll remain tied to the tree.

Enrico
Rant on – do what you want to me.

Pedrisco points to Galván.

Pedrisco
Him as well.

Galván
That's me a goner.

Pedrisco
Every man has the face he deserves, they say –
You must have done some ugly deeds –
Come on – move – tie them up.

He roars at Enrico.

Over to that tree – move.

Enrico
So this is what Heaven's in store for me.

They tie Enrico, and then Galván, to a tree.

Pedrisco
You next –

Galván
Go gentle with me –

Pedrisco
Blindfold their eyes, both of them.

Galván
Well, this is a right pickle.
Listen, lord and master –
We share a vocation –
I've served time in the thieving trade.

Pedrisco
So justice is done and seen to be done –
That will make the hangman happy.

First Bandit
That's them nicely trussed and ready for stuffing.

Pedrisco
Fetch us our bows and gather the arrows –
Twenty-four should suffice – waste not, want not.
We'll bury the lot in each body.

First Bandit
Get started.

Pedrisco speaks quietly to one of the Bandits.

Pedrisco
All for show – no one's to touch them.

First Bandit
I think the boss has made their acquaintance.

Pedrisco

We'll shove off, and leave them like that.

Pedrisco and the Bandits exit.

SCENE SIX

Galván

They're going to riddle us with arrows.

Enrico

And I won't show the slightest worry.

Galván

I can feel my stomach torn asunder.

Enrico

Christ, avenge me.
I'd like to repent,
But when I want to, I can't.

Dressed as a hermit, with a cross and rosary, Paulo enters.

Paulo

In this garb, I'll test this man –
See if he thinks of the God he's insulted.
God be praised.

Enrico

Praised eternal.

Paulo

Fortune's hit you hard –
Face up to that bravely.

Enrico

It's hit below the belt –
Who is it speaks to me?

66

Paulo

A monk –
I live in the desert where you will die.

Enrico

That lifts the heart for sure.
What is it you want from me?

Paulo

You believe in God, I take it –
Would you like to confess?

Enrico

Forget that scenario, Father –
Or whatever it is you are.

Paulo

What are you saying?
Do you not believe in Christ?

Enrico

I do, yes.

Paulo

I think not –
You refuse the last sacrament.
Why won't you receive it?

Enrico

Because I don't want it.

Paulo speaks in aside.

Paulo

Just as I predicted.

He turns to Enrico.

Can you not see they'll kill you soon?

Enrico

Would you shut your mouth, pal, and leave me be?

67

If those gentlemen want to thieve my life,
Then here I am, waiting for them.

Paulo

My soul does not know where to turn.

Enrico

Galván, I wonder if Celia – my old lady –
Is she about her business?

Galván

This slight predicament I find myself in –
Do you think I give a tinker's curse?

Paulo

Turn your mind to higher things.

Enrico

Father dear, you are beginning to irk me.

Paulo

My prayers – they offend you?

Enrico

They weary me.
If I were not a little tied up now,
You'd feel my boot kick you to kingdom come.

Paulo

You're on the point of death – beware –

Enrico

And I am worn out waiting –

Galván

Father, I'll confess –
I'm good as dead already.

Enrico

This blindfold – take it from me, Father.

Paulo

I will, of course, yes.

He removes the blindfold from Enrico and Galván.

Enrico

Thank Christ I can see at last.

Galván

Me as well.

Paulo

Just in time to catch a glimpse of your killers.

Bandits enter with rifles and crossbows.

Enrico

Well, what's stopping you?

Pedrisco

Celio, blast his heart out.

Enrico

Come on, you pack of cowards.
Here is my heart – fire.

Pedrisco

This time finish the job.

Paulo

Wait – harm him and you harm me.
Son, you are a sinner –

Enrico

The world's worst – I know –

Paulo

I want what's best for you – that's all.
Confess to God –

Enrico

I've said no – shove your preaching –

Paulo

Then let my tears blind me in such torrents
That they drown my soul – I do not trust God.

Strip myself of these holy vestments –
They should not cover this sinful body.
My stomach sickens at that hypocrisy.
I am like a snake shedding its skin –
I hide beneath this sacred habit
What it is I am – a cruel sinner.
Hang these robes over there – they say to the world,
Here he left us hanging, Paulo who disgraced us.
Give me the dagger – give me the sword –
Remove the cross – here is hope abandoned.
Christ shed his hallowed blood for nothing.
Free those men. Free them immediately.

The Bandits untie and release Enrico and Galván.

Enrico

I can't believe what I witness.

Galván

Thanks be to God in Heaven.

Enrico

I want the truth – what's happening?

Paulo

I am Paulo, a hermit –
Fifteen years in exile from his loved country,
Serving the Lord ten years on this dark mountain.

Enrico

Aren't you the lucky boy?

Paulo

When I asked God what fate I'd suffer,
He sent an angel through clouds of gold and silver,
Ripping them apart – Be still my soul, still.
Endure misfortune! He told me take heed,
Go to the city, find Enrico,
Son of Anareto, well known in Naples.

Study his words, look to his deeds,
If Enrico goes to Heaven, so do you,
But if it's Hell, then Hell is waiting.
I hoped this Enrico would be a saint –
I hoped in vain – I went and saw you,
The worst man in the world –
And I would share your fate. So be it –
I took the vestments from my back,
Fell in with this squad of desperate men.
I wanted to test you – do you remember God,
In your pain and panic, next to death?
All in vain – I am raw red, my soul bereft –
For God has sentenced it to Hell.

Enrico

Mere mortals cannot comprehend, Paulo,
The words God puts in an angel's mouth.
Despair has taken you by the hand,
So you look for revenge against God's word.
You're fighting a battle you're bound to lose.
But he's spared you, I see – he wants you saved.
Ask – he's always merciful – always.
I'm the most hateful of human beings –
But I do hope that I will be saved –
Hope everlasting, hope eternal,
Not in myself, nor in my doings
But in the mercy and pity of Christ.
Paulo, you've lost your bearings entirely –
Be happy, be content on this mountain,
The two of us leading life as it comes
As long as it's ours for the taking.
If Heaven is barred to the both of us –
We'll drown our sorrows just as we share them.
I believe above all in God's mercy.
It knocks justice into a corner.

Paulo
You bring me a bit of comfort.

He speaks to Pedrisco.

Enrico
I left behind me one thing I love –
My father – my loved father.
They will gut me if I go back to Naples –
Paulo, I have to save him or die trying.
One of your boys must come with me.

Paulo
Pedrisco's your man – he knows what's what.

Pedrisco
I'd started to think you'd nudged me aside.

Paulo
Give Enrico the best sword –
Take the fastest horses –
You'll be back within two hours.

Galván speaks to Pedrisco.

Galván
On the mountains I'll be your right-hand man –

Pedrisco
And my skull will leave my shoulders
Because of your badness –

Enrico
Farewell, friend.

Paulo
And friends we'll stay – I'll show you proof.

They embrace.

Enrico
I may be foul – but I have faith in God.

Paulo
I have none left – and my sins are legion.

Enrico
God hears – and he has mercy.

The voice of the Shepherd is heard singing as the prison takes shape.

Shepherd
Our flesh is weak
And it falters –
God looks away,
Is his love lost?
No, God is mercy,
God is mercy, mercy,
Love is mercy, mercy.

SCENE SEVEN

A prison with bars at the rear through which a street can be seen.

Pedrisco
Any more bright ideas?

Enrico
Why the whinging?

Pedrisco
Why am I whinging?
Can I not shed a tear for my innocent self?
Here I am punished for another man's sins.

Enrico
Be like myself – I suffer too –
But I keep a stiff upper lip –

Pedrisco

They say the one who sins should pay –
And I believe them – I'm blameless.
Why me, Lord – oh, why me?

Enrico

Pedrisco, put a sock in it.

Pedrisco

I'll put a drawerful of socks in it, pal –
But a hungry corpse would sing for its supper.
Right – had my say – stay silent as the grave.

Enrico

So you think we're in prison for life?

Pedrisco

That is indeed what I do think –
From the day and hour we were carted in.

Enrico

Our luck will change, I'm certain.

SCENE EIGHT

Celia and Lidora enter on the street.
Celia stops in front of the prison window.

Celia

Prisons don't take a wrinkle out of me –
We don't have to enter hand in hand –

Lidora

I'm your dogsbody – I must go with you –

Enrico

A bit of hush – this is Celia.

Pedrisco

Celia who?

74

Enrico

The woman who worships me more than life.
Celia, my beauty – my darling.

Celia speaks in aside to Lidora.

Celia

I'm done for – Enrico's called me.

She goes to the window.

Enrico, my friend.

Pedrisco

Friend – she calls you just a friend?
Not ripping her skirt off, is she?

Enrico

Celia, I'd lost hope of help –

Celia

I bring news to ease your worries.

Enrico

See – ease my worries –

Pedrisco

Luck shines out of your every orifice.

Celia

Your cares will be gone by tomorrow –
That's when they execute you.

Enrico

I shouldn't have to hear the like –
Celia, why are you so calm –

Pedrisco

This will be good – I bank on it –

Celia

I am now a wedded woman –

Enrico
What?

Pedrisco
She is now a wedded woman.

Enrico
Who to, Celia?

Celia
Lisandro – he's a wonderful catch.

Liadora
He's a dwarf.

Celia
He's a rich one.

Enrico
I will slice his single ball off.

Celia
Forget such stuff – make peace with God –
That's what should be bothering you.

Lidora
Celia, get a move on.

Enrico
I'm losing my mind. Celia – Celia –

Celia
I've a million things on my plate –

Pedrisco
She's good that one – she is a panic –

Celia
I know what it is you require of me –
Arrange a Mass to be said for your soul.
Consider it done – God go with you.

Enrico

If I could break through these bars –

Lidora

Celia, don't listen to any more laments –
Let's clear out of this place.

Enrico

That I should have to put up with this –
Have you seen the like for cruelty?
How dare you do this to me, tramp?
I will smash you, whore, to smithereens.
You will feel the naked ire of my fist.

Celia

Lidora, he will kill me –

Lidora

You frighten her, Enrico, you always have –

Enrico

It's what she wanted – what all women wanted –

Lidora

No, we want the boot on the other foot.
It is now – you feel fear – fear for your life.
Goodbye, big man, swing gently on your rope.

Celia and Lidora exit.

Enrico

Jesus Christ, do I endure this affront?
Why can I not bend this iron?
Why can't I pull these bars to pieces?

Pedrisco

The guards are coming.

Enrico

Let them.

Two Wardens enter.

First Warden
>Listen to this thieving git –
>Maybe he's losing his mind –

Enrico
>I'll beat that bitch into a pulp –
>These chains will do the job before I die –

Pedrisco
>For Christ's sake, stop.

First Warden
>Hold him down – kill him – kill him –

Enrico attacks a Warden.

Enrico
>You cowards and curs, do you see now
>What a jealous man does to his jailers?

Second Warden
>He's struck me – I'm on the floor –

Enrico
>Where are you running to, bastards?

Pedrisco
>You've killed a guard –

Voice (*off*)
>Kill him – kill him –

Enrico
>What would you know about killing?
>They might have swiped the sword from me –
>I'll pay them back with the lash of the chain.
>Why are you scurrying away from me?

Pedrisco
>The noise and racket has wakened himself –
>The prison governor.

The Governor enters with Wardens.

Governor
What in the hell is this pandemonium?
Stop it now – what's happening?

First Warden
This thief's taken Fidelio's life.

Governor
If I didn't know you swing tomorrow,
I would set you as a fine example.
My dagger would rip your dirtbag belly.

Enrico
Look at my eyes – there's lightning in them.
Think for one minute, you jumped-up jailbird,
That I have respect for the likes of you?
I'd drink your blood and eat your flesh –
Carve it slowly limb by limb –
I would still be hungry for more revenge.

Governor
Ten o'clock tomorrow he'll meet his maker –
See if he's as fierce facing the hangman.
Weigh him down with another chain.

Enrico
Chains, chains, more clatter of chains –
The music of all my mischievous deeds.
I hear them singing in the rattle of chains.

Governor
Throw him into the darkest cell –

Enrico
That is quite remarkably apt –
The man who'd shoot God should not look to Heaven.

They take him away.

Pedrisco

Poor soul, Enrico – a sad case.

First Warden

This dead man, he's a damn sight sadder.
He's had his brains dashed all over the floor.
Well may he curse that bastard's cruel chains.

He exits, hauling Pedrisco with him.

Pedrisco

I smell food – where are you taking me?
Out for a little dinner?

The Warden kicks Pedrisco in the mouth.

Warden

Eat this – That will shut you up, pig.

SCENE NINE

As Enrico is roughly tied in chains the voice of the Shepherd is heard singing.

Shepherd

Listen and learn
From lives of the saints –
They sinned most gravely.
Now they are saved –
They dwell in the peace
Of Paradise.
Ask St Peter,
Apostle Matthew,
Francis of Assisi,
Scorning the sacraments,
Received five wounds
And gloried Christ –
Long led astray,

Perfumed in Palestine,
Mary of Magdalena
Was called by God.
They dwell in the peace
Of Paradise.
They dwell in the peace
Of Paradise.

Enrico is now completely chained and alone.

SCENE TEN

Enrico
The bold Enrico, this is your end,
Lost in the darkness.
Time to stand up and show your mettle.

Voice (*off*)
Enrico –

Enrico
Who's calling me?
It's sent a shiver down my spine –

Voice
Enrico –

Enrico
That voice leaves me shaking –
My hair's standing on end –

Voice
Enrico –

Enrico
What's happening? I'm weak as a woman –

Voice
Enrico –

Enrico

My soul is stiff worrying –
Whose voice turns me to ice?

Voice

Enrico –

Enrico

It keeps on and on calling.
I am shocked to be such a child.
That voice – it's coming from over there.
Some pitiful prisoner held in chains?

The Devil appears, invisible to Enrico.

Devil

Poor Enrico – in deep disgrace –
I'm here to set you free, Enrico.

Enrico

You are a voice coming from Hell knows where.
Who are you? What are you? How can I believe –

Devil

Very soon you will see me.

The Devil appears to Enrico in the form of a shadow.

Enrico

And I wish now that I couldn't.

Devil

Feel no fear.

Enrico

A cold sweat's pouring out of my veins.

Devil

From this day throughout the earth,
They will know of your name.

Enrico

I'm not the man you think – don't come near me.

Devil

I'm giving you a chance – take it –

Enrico

My heart beats like the hammers of Hell –
Stop.

At the Devil's signal, a door opens in the wall.

Devil

Do you see this door?

Enrico

Yes.

Devil

Walk through it – you'll be out of prison.

Enrico

Who are you?

Devil

Walk now – don't ask who I am.
I'm in prison too – trying to free you.

Enrico

Will I make my getaway – I will.
I'm looking death straight in the face.
I'll do a runner – What holds me back?

Voices are heard singing.

Voices

Do not fear
These prison walls,
They shall melt
And free your soul.
Free yourself,
Remain enslaved.
Do not fear
These prison walls.

Enrico

This advice has stopped me dead –
The opposite of what you said.
I'm told I'm better off in jail –

Devil

A dream to turn your head astray –
A fearful, pure illusion.

Enrico

Stay here and die – no, get away –
You're right – show me how –

Voices are heard singing.

Voices

Free yourself,
Remain enslaved.
Do not fear
These prison walls.
They shall melt
And free your soul –
Free yourself,
Remain enslaved.

Enrico

If I go, I die – if I stay, I'll live.
That's the voice I hear singing.

Devil

So you do not wish to leave?

Enrico

It's better to stay put, I'd say.

Devil

All you're fit for is to die in jail –
A craven coward with shit for brains.
Fate will clean its arse with you. Farewell.

The Devil exits.

SCENE ELEVEN

Enrico is alone.

Enrico
> The shadow vanished into air –
> Was I blind or did I see what I saw?
> Can I not leave? Yes, I can – can leave.
> How? I have to die. The voice frightened me.
> Never felt that before till I felt it then.

The Governor enters with the sentence.

Enrico
> What do you want?

Governor
> How he handles himself at the worst of times –
> That's the mark of a man. What are you?
> Will you listen to this?

Enrico
> Speak out.

The Governor speaks in aside.

Governor
> Not a flicker on his face.

He reads.

In the suits between the following two parties, His
Majesty's own prosecutor, in his absence, and the
other, the prisoner Enrico, for crimes of which he is
accused – being a delinquent, a murderer and many
other charges. We rule that we must pronounce him
guilty. He is thus condemned to be taken from this
prison where he is held, a noose tied to his neck and
with criers announcing his crimes before him, may
he be led to the public square, where there will be a

gallows, high above the floor, on which he will hang until he is dead. And let no person dare remove him without our licence or orders. And thus we rule this definitive judgement, and so we pronounce and command it.

Enrico
You have the nerve to tell me this?

Governor
What is it you're saying?

Enrico
Look at these arms, you ignorant idiot,
I could knock you into the middle of next week –

Governor
Save your bluster and your big talk.
Only one thing matters now, Enrico.
You must make your peace with God.

Enrico
You preach as you pass judgement, do you?
You creeping Jesus, I'll swing for you.

Governor
May the Devil see his own in you.

He exits.

SCENE TWELVE

Enrico is alone.

Enrico
Sentenced to lonely, lousy death –
Two hours left of my existence.
I'll die here when I could have walked.

A Warden enters.

Warden

Two friars of St Francis wait outside –
They want to hear your confession.

Enrico

Well, they'll wait till Hell freezes over.
Tell the monks to crawl back to their convents,
Or I'll break their teeth with this iron chain.

Warden

You're facing death – remember that.

Enrico

I'll die without penance – I'm my own master.
Whatever I've done on my head be it.

Warden

Aren't you the fine upstanding fellow?

Enrico

I've spoken and I won't repeat it.
See these chains – they'll be wrapped round your trousers
If I lose my head once and for all.

Warden

So you won't confess?

Enrico

Why bother? It's a waste of breath.
Why dredge up all my dirty sins?
Even I can't recall the slings and arrows
I've hurled in God's direction – let them lie,
Best not to brood on such dark matters.

Warden

If you won't see the friars,
You might speak to this man.

87

Anareto enters.

Your grey hairs may crack this hard diamond.

The Warden exits.

SCENE THIRTEEN

Anareto
Enrico, my son, I have always adored –
It breaks my heart to see you in this state –
You're crippled as I am with your chains.
I've left my bed to lean on this stick
And come here for a reason – one reason only.

Enrico
My kind father –

Anareto
'Father' – is that name fit for me, Enrico?

Enrico
Can a man say that to his son?

Anareto
A son who does not believe in God –
He has no right calling me father.

Enrico
How can you come out with this, Father?

Anareto
You are no longer my son.
You don't obey my law.
We are both on our own.

Enrico
I do not understand you.

88

Anareto

Enrico, Enrico –
I try to curb your wild imaginings –
I tell you surely you're going to die.
Today you will be executed,
And you will not confess.
This pride is preparation for Hell, Enrico.
You might as well knock a mountain senseless –
Use your fists to flatten a lump of rock –
It's you that ends up smashed and broken.
You will die today – that dice is thrown –
So confess your sins to good God.
You will be forgiven, then death is life,
Life eternal in the love of Christ.
If you stay my boy, do as I tell you.
If not – I am torn in two – but still I say
You must not call yourself my son –
And I do not know you.

Enrico

All will be well, Father – seeing you suffer,
That's touched my soul more than all my troubles.
I will admit to all my errors,
Confess my crimes and kiss the foot
Of every dog and devil.
To prove once and for all my faith in you,
It's enough you ask, and I'll obey,
My dearest father, light of my life.

Anareto

Then you are my son again.

Enrico

I don't want to make you cross.

Anareto

We'll go and you can tell your sins.

Enrico
I'm frightened you're going to leave me.

Anareto
And I'm frightened to lose you.

Enrico
Look at your eyes that were bright as stars,
Lovely as mirrors that shine,
Now they are starved of light.

Anareto
Come on, lad.

Enrico
I'm going to die – and I'm very scared.

Anareto
I've lost my soul and reason.

Enrico
Wait, please, Father – please –

Anareto
Child, my heart's broken –

Enrico
Citadel of the stars and high mountains,
Hear me, merciful Almighty God.
Greater than grains of sand in the ocean,
My sins are many and monstrous to see,
But God, your mercy is ever greater.
You shed your innocent blood to save us,
Nailed to a cross for the sins of Adam.
Allow me be worthy of just one drop.
Beautiful Virgin, Aurora of Heaven,
Angels surround you, refuge of sinners –
Sinner I am – pray for me.
Remind your son, His Holy Majesty,

He once was a pilgrim walking our earth.
To him do we cry, begging forgiveness,
Poor banished children of our mother Eve,
Saviour most selfless, Christ our Redeemer.
Now that I stand in the light of his reason,
Tell him I'd go through a thousand deaths,
Rather than harm or offend him.

Enrico's chains start to fall from him.

Anareto
They want us to get along.

Enrico
Mercy, my Lord – grant me mercy.
That is all I can say to you.

Anareto
Come with me, son.

Enrico
I hear you say son, my tears fall in torrents.
Father, don't leave me till my breath turns to bone.

Anareto
Don't be frightened – God goes with you.

Enrico
He will, for he is a torrent of mercy,
And I am dead already.

Anareto
Courage – courage –

Enrico
In God I trust, Father.
Lead me where they'll take the life you first gave.

Anareto leads Enrico to his execution, giving him a crucifix.
  There is sacred music.
  A priest blesses Enrico and he is given the Eucharist.
  Enrico clutches the crucifix.
  He asks all to forgive him.
  Tears soak his cheeks.
  The execution takes place.
  The Shepherd's voice is heard singing.

Shepherd
  A lamb has been lost –
  My master, my Lord –
  He longs to see you
  Return to his fields.

  Two winged angels appear.
    There is celestial music and extraordinary light.
    They carry Enrico to Paradise.
    The Shepherd's voice is heard singing as darkness descends.

  Beg forgiveness
  If you did offend.
  Mercy is waiting,
  Mercy for the world.

  Paulo appears in the darkness, alone.
    The Shepherd's voice sings.

Shepherd
  Lamb that is lost,
  What do you flee from?

  Paulo joins in duet with the Shepherd.

Duet

Lamb that is lost,
Come back to me.
Lamb that is lost,
Come back to me.

Paulo is alone.

Paulo

I've left behind the men I command
And raced to this dark mountainside.
I'll rest in the shade of this green willow
And see if I can forget my past sorrow.
The fountain whispers among the rocks,
Pleasing the flowers and the creatures of air –
Give me solace too, ease my sore soul
With your cold water of chanting voices.
Sweet birds in the fragrant bunch of thyme,
Lost in the reeds and the lonely rushes,
Sing me your gentle innocent song.
Broken with sorrow, leaden with worries,
On this green grass tattered with dew,
I want distraction from all my ills,
The pain of the punishments I face –
They lead me to my fearful end.

He lies down to sleep.
  *The Shepherd arrives, unmaking the crown of
flowers.*
  The Shepherd sings.

Shepherd

I have come back,
I am the shepherd
Who minded the sheep,
Innocent, happy.
One day the finest
Ran from the flock,

Drenching my eyes
With sourest tears.
Happiness turned
Into cold sorrow –
All that was pleasant
Had passed and gone.
I wove these flowers
Into a crown
That she took and
Tore into pieces,
Lost in the world
Of trick and trade,
Far from the one
Who most loves her.
I now dismantle
This diadem –
Revenge on her
Who destroyed it.
Lamb that is lost,
What do you flee from?
Lamb that is lost,
Come back to me.

Paulo

Would you not receive her were she to return?

The Shepherd sings.

Shepherd

Through the fearful forest
I wander after her –
Brambles tear my feet,
Broken and bloodied.
I go to my master
To tell this news –
How shall I speak,
Unless with tears,

A torrent of tears,
A torrent of tears?
Lamb that is lost,
What do you flee from?
Lamb that is lost,
Come back to me.

The Shepherd exits.

SCENE FIFTEEN

Paulo is alone.

Paulo

His song is the story of my own life –
What do I make of this shepherd?
His words are a dream none may explain.

There is extraordinary light.

Paulo

That light burns more bright than rays of the sun.

Music plays as two angels are seen taking Enrico's soul to Heaven.

Music plays through the celestial spheres –
I see two angels deliver a soul,
Full of grace, to divine Paradise.
Fair soul, most fortunate a thousand times,
Today you go where your labours have ended.
Fruits of the earth, flora and fauna,
Do you see the sky break itself open?
Dispersing the clouds of deepest darkness.
Happy soul, ascend to glorious Heaven.
Shame on the man who spurns you, pure soul.

Galván enters.

Galván

Paulo, I'm here to give you fair warning –
There's a whole militia descending the mountain,
Armed to the teeth, looking solely for you.
Unless you intend to give up the ghost,
We have to run – that's all we can do.
You can hear the drums and see the banners.
If you wait you won't see another day.

Paulo

Who brought them here?

Galván

The poor people – unless I'm much mistaken.
They hate how we threaten them in the mountains.
They've gathered from every townland and parish.

Paulo

So – kill them.

Galván

What? You're going to face them down?

Paulo

You don't know who Paulo really is –

Galván

I do know we are in serious danger –

Paulo

One true man takes on a thousand scum.

Galván

Their drums are beating – can you hear them?

Paulo

Silence – have no fear they'll harm you.

Before I took to the penitent life,
I served my time as a good soldier.

A Judge and Villagers enter.

Judge
The crimes you committed on this mountain –
Today you'll account for each and every one.

Paulo
My heart is cold though my blood's on fire –
I have become Enrico.

Villager
Give yourselves up, thieves – Get them –

Galván
Better off dead – I'll make a run for it –

Galván runs away.
The Villagers follow him.
Paulo begins to stab them.

Paulo
You bastards have the advantage –
Two hundred of you against our twenty.
Come on then – do your damned worst.

Judge
He's getting away down the mountain.

Paulo falls down the mountain, covered in blood,
screaming.

Paulo
I am not dead – I am alive –
Still breath in me – I am not finished –

Pedrisco enters and sees the fallen Paulo.

Pedrisco
The mighty Paulo, lying in a heap –

Christ look down on this misfortune.
It's Pedrisco, my own Paulo.

Paulo
Pedrisco, take me in your arms.
Now I'm dying – tell me, my friend –
Enrico – what happened to him – let me hear.

Pedrisco
They hung him in the square at Naples.

Paulo
So he stood condemned and burns in Hell –

Pedrisco
He died a Christian gentleman,
As he died we could all hear music
In the divine, seraphic air.
An even bigger miracle happened then –
We witnessed two winged angels appear.
They fetched Enrico's soul to Paradise.

Paulo
Enrico – evil seed of the Devil – the worst man –

Pedrisco
It shocks you, Paulo, that God shows mercy?

Paulo
It was another's soul – not Enrico's –
That's what you saw, Pedrisco – a trick.

Pedrisco
Enrico and God are the best of mates.
Beg the Lord to forgive you.

Paulo
How can he do that to a man like myself
Who has offended him in every way?

Pedrisco
How can you doubt it? He forgave Enrico –

Paulo
God is all mercy –

Pedrisco
You say it –

Paulo
But not to men such as I am.
Give me your hands – I'm dying.

Pedrisco
He's dead, poor man, pierced and broken.
Enrico and himself, they've swapped their souls –
The evil one now ensconsed in Heaven,
The good man doubts his way into Hell.
I'll cover his most unhappy corpse.
Green willow branches – they'll do the job.
Who are these people coming here?

SCENE SEVENTEEN

The Judge and Villagers enter, with Galván captured.
Pedrisco has hidden Paulo's dead body.

Judge
We've been very careless if we let Paulo go.

Villager
I saw him fall from the high rocks,
Rolling down the mountain, all full of blood.

Judge
That man there, catch him.

Pedrisco
Pedrisco, this time you're in for it.

A Villager points to Galván.

Villager
That's a crony of Paulo's – his partner in crime.

Galván
No, I was Enrico's – you lying toad.

Pedrisco
Same as myself, wee brother Galván.

He speaks to Galván in an aside.

For the love of Christ, don't squeal on me.

Judge
Tell us where your boss is hiding –

Pedrisco
No point searching him out when he's dead.

Judge
How can he be dead?

Pedrisco
That is how I found him, sir,
His many wounds were fatal.
This very spot – he died in agony.

Judge
Where is he?

Pedrisco
I laid his corpse behind these boughs.

He is about to move the boughs aside when Paulo, in flames, appears.

Paulo
You asked to see Paulo, then gaze on Paulo.
His body is aflame, eaten by vipers.
I blame no one for the torments I suffer.

I myself am pain – the source of my pain.
Satan took the shape of a holy angel –
And I swallowed whole his damned deceit.
Now I am damned and descend to the pit,
To the dark abyss – endure the pangs of Hell.
God's curse on the pair who gave me birth –
God's curse on myself – my doubt and despair.

He sinks as fire flames from the earth.

Judge
The ways of God are exceedingly strange.

Galván
That man is a pity –

Pedrisco
And Enrico basks in the glow of God.

Judge
Look on this and learn –
Let that be your punishment.
I set you both free as birds.

Pedrisco
Sir, may you live for ever and ever.
So, Brother Galván, we've survived that scrape –
What plans are you hatching here on in?

Galván
I am quite tempted to become a saint.

Pedrisco
I won't put money on many miracles.

Galván
Have faith in God.

Pedrisco
True – look what happens to lads who don't.

Galván
We'll head to Naples – tell all about this.

Pedrisco
Hard enough to credit, but it's a true story –
Read about it in what religion you fancy.
They all have their tales of being damned by despair
And may God protect you, till he comes calling.

The End.